Santa's Christmas with a Mask

By
Divya Mohan

Art by
Hend Moharram

LETTER TO
Official 🎅 Santa

Dear Santa,

My name is Milo,
I am 4 years old.
I have been NICE.
My biggest wish:
Lots of Candies.

Thank you Santa

Author: Divya Mohan
Illustrator: Hend Moharram
Editor: Seb Jenkins
Proof reader: Chrissy Cutting

Published by: Value Buds

ISBN: 978-0-6485321-7-0 (paperback)
© The Value Buds 2020

Visit www.authordivya.com for more information.

To my little daughter, Ridhi.
You adapted well to all the changes that
year 2020 brought
to you.

Little Mili and Milo were so excited that they posted their letters to Santa in July!

But little did they know that
the letters were lost in the postbox
for such a long time...

Would they reach Santa in time
for Christmas day?

Far away in the heart of the North Pole, Santa sat and watched the news.

"There's a virus in town,"
the reporter said,
as Santa jumped up,
almost losing his shoes.

"A lockdown in the North Pole—
Stage four restrictions apply!"
That meant that Santa couldn't
pack his sleigh—let alone fly!

No one could leave their homes
but for medicine and groceries.

This news had Santa feeling so nervous,
he was weak at the knees!

How would he
get his gifts all packed
and ready for Christmas?
He even had to
shut down the toy factory,
oh what a fuss!

Santa waited patiently for
his factory's reopening time.
He would have to employ extra elves
to meet the Xmas deadline.

Time ticked by
and before long it was August,
just four months to go.

Yet lockdown continued
as Santa looked out at the snow.

"Oh dear," he cried.
"Whatever are we going to do?"
"To be ready in time for Christmas,
so many presents are due!"

Santa and his elves
had to start working soon.
The letters were piling up!
Was Christmas doomed?

There was no other choice,
but to start work now!
And Santa suddenly thought
that he knew exactly how!

He and the elves would simply work from home, Getting through the presents without needing to roam.

Santa immediately set up a video call with his top elves. They then came up with a Christmas plan between themselves.

Letter to Official Santa

Dear Santa,

My name is Milo.
I am 4 years old.
I have been NICE.
My biggest wish:
Lots of Candies.

Thank you

They started making
toys at home,
but what about
all the candy?
All the sweet shops
were closed
and that wasn't very handy!

Santa called up his old friend
Mr. Choc, the candy factory owner.
He said that the factory was closed too,
oh what a disaster!

Fortunately, the candy makers were working from home, too. They took Santa's order and said: "We'll deliver it all to you!"

Two days before Christmas
and they had made so many toys—
Candies, chocolates, books, and activities
for all the good girls and boys.

But then Santa received a last-minute
knock at the door,
The postman had a huge pile of letters—
and he said there were more!

Nearly half of the children
had not yet had their presents made.

"Good heavens,
we need a
miracle now,"
Santa fervently
prayed.

After a video meeting
with the chief elves,
a plan was hatched.
They ordered thousands of
gifts online,
next-day dispatched.

Within 24 hours,

the **gifts** had arrived at the North Pole.
Just in time for Santa to go!
That meant no lumps of coal!

Then disaster struck,
as all international flights were banned.
"Does this mean that
reindeer delivery can no longer stand?"

Santa called up The President
and asked for special permission.
"All the kids are waiting for us
to deliver their presents
on our Xmas mission!"

The President said:
"You can fly your sleigh, but
only if you wear a mask!"
"Ho Ho! Of course,
Mr. President," Santa said.
"You need only ask!"

1NEWS
LIVE

BREAKING NEWS No Airplanes will fly from tonight
COVID OUTBREAK • COVID OUTBREAK • COVID OUT 10:00

Santa had already handmade
enough masks for his team.
He made sure he had everything,
then took off like a stream!

The next morning,
Mili and Milo woke up with a feeling of glee.

To find that their presents
were placed safely under the tree!

Merry Christmas!

Hello, little girls and boys,
how was your year 2020?

Did you learn new things
and have online classes?

Did you wear masks
or stay home?

How did you feel?

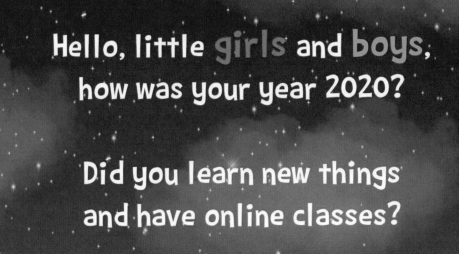

What is your biggest wish this Christmas?

You can write to me at divya@authordivya.com
or @authordivyamohan (FB and IG).

Do you know what is my biggest wish?
It is to know how much you loved this book!
Would you write a review for me on Amazon?
I will look forward to reading it :).

With lots of Love,
Divya

The new normal practices

WEAR A MASK

WASH HANDS

SOCIAL DISTANCE

STAY HOME WHEN SICK

Have a safe Christmas

Made in the USA
Monee, IL
01 December 2020